E

W9-COM-947

Buzaak Chinie

The Porcelain Goat

A Traditional Afghan Folk Tale
Told and Illustrated by

Asma Salehi

◇◇◇

Long River Press
San Francisco

First Edition
Published in the United States of America by
Long River Press
360 Swift Avenue, Suite 48
South San Francisco, CA 94080
www.longriverpress.com

Editor: Chris Robyn
Book design: Nathan Grover

The CIP record for this title is on file at the United States Library of Congress
Printed in the United States of America

To my son Noah Nadi, my mother Razia Salehi, and my grandmother Zahra Mohammadi

Once upon a time there was a goat with porcelain-white hair. Her name was Buzaak Chinie and she had three kids: Angak, Bangak, and Kulola Sangak. Buzaak Chinie preferred to call them by their nicknames: Stubby, Clumsy, and Whiney. They all lived in a house deep in the forest. Each day, Buzaak Chinie left the house to take a jug of milk to the blacksmith. In return, the blacksmith gave Buzaak Chinie food. Each morning before she left to visit the blacksmith, she reminded the kids not to open the door for anyone: "This is a big forest, young ones," she would tell them.

One morning, not long after Buzaak Chinie had left for the blacksmith's shop, the kids were playing in the house when they heard a knock at the door. The three goats suddenly froze, scared. They huddled together in a corner of the room. The knocking continued. Whiney, who was the oldest, went to the door and asked, her voice quivering, "Wh-Wh-Who's there?" A deep voice growled on the other side of the door: "Hello little goat. This is Uncle Big Wolf. I have come from the faraway jungle for a visit. Please open the door." Whiney looked at Stubby and Clumsy still huddled together in the corner. They both looked very scared. Big Wolf knocked again. Whiney, in her strongest voice, said to him, "Our mother told us not to open the door while she was gone." But Big Wolf did not give up so easily. In his sweetest voice he said, "Don't be afraid little one; you can open the door for your uncle." Whiney did not know what to do. She told Big Wolf, "Go away! Come back when our mother is home."

Big Wolf simply smiled to himself, turned, and left.

A short while later, Big Wolf returned, and knocked on the door once again. He cleared his throat and said in his sweetest voice: "It is Buzaak Chinie my darlings. Open the door! I have a surprise for you!" So relieved were they to have their mother home at last, Stubby, Clumsy, and Whiney ran to the door. They did not even think to ask whether it might be Big Wolf. As the door opened on its hinges, Big Wolf pushed his way in. The goats were petrified, but all they could see were two rows of sharp, white teeth right in front of them! In the blink of an eye, Big Wolf caught them and ate them whole! There they sat, frightened and shivering, in Big Wolf's dark tummy. Big Wolf, meanwhile, ambled over to rest under a tree.

As Big Wolf was resting, Buzaak Chinie returned home with food from the blacksmith. She was shocked to discover that her front door was wide open. She went into the house calling, "Stubby! Clumsy! Whiney! Where are you?" But there was no answer. She dropped the basket of food and raced into the forest, calling the young goats by name. In no time at all she had reached the swamp. She pounded her hooves desperately against a tree next to a pond, trying to get the attention of Short-Tempered Alligator, who lived there. Suddenly, there were ripples on the pond's surface and a huge alligator poked his head above the water with a frown. "Who is knocking at my door, shaking dirt on my floor, and raising my temper?" grumbled Short-Tempered Alligator. "It is I, Buzaak Chinie." She said. "I am searching for my kids. Have you seen them?" Short-Tempered Alligator growled, "No, I have not seen your goats. I have been sleeping here at the bottom of this pond. You should go ask Striped Tiger."

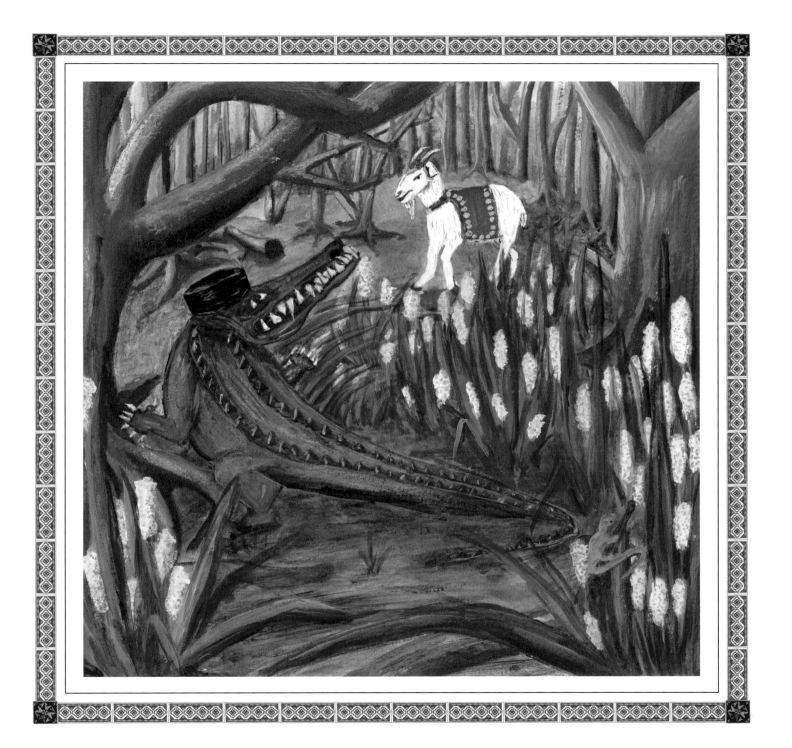

Buzaak Chinie thanked Short-Tempered Alligator and raced off to find Striped Tiger. Seeing his house in the distance, she approached cautiously and knocked at his door. Listening carefully, Buzaak Chinie could hear a loud yawn, which suddenly turned into a load roar. Striped Tiger exclaimed, "Who is knocking at my door, shaking dirt on my floor, and giving me a hard time?" "It is I, Buzaak Chinie." She said. "Have you seen my kids? I can't find them anywhere!" Striped Tiger opened his door and looked at Buzzak Chinie. "No, I have not seen them," he said. "I was sleeping here all day. Why don't you ask Yellow Lion?"

Buzaak Chinie thanked Striped Tiger and then ran off to find Yellow Lion. Soon, she found him resting outside his grand tent. Yellow Lion did not sleep in a house. Rather, he slept under a tent as he feared no other creature (he was King of the beasts, after all). Buzaak Chinie approached him and said, "Yellow Lion, it is I, Buzaak Chinie. I am searching for my three kids, Clumsy, Stubby, and Whiney. Have you seen them?" Yellow Lion shook his head slowly and said, "Sorry, Buzaak Chinie, I have not seen them." Yellow Lion paused for a moment, then said, "I think you are looking in the wrong place, if you know what I mean. Find that troublemaker Big Wolf and you may find your kids." Buzaak Chinie caught the wisdom in Yellow Lion's words. Though frightened, she thanked Yellow Lion and set off to find Big Wolf.

13

The sun was setting when Buzaak Chinie finally found Big Wolf's house. She knocked at his door, but there was no answer. She knocked again. But Big Wolf was resting outside, under a nearby tree. Without even bothering to turn around, he growled, "Who is knocking on my door at this hour! Shaking dirt on my floor, and ruining my nap, too!" "Where are my goats!" demanded Buzaak Chinie. Big Wolf merely laughed. "Ha! Ha! Ha!" He gloated, patting his belly, "They are right here! Would you care to join them? Too bad I'm so full already!" Buzaak Chinie was shaking with anger. "You will not get away with this! At first light, we shall meet at Warrior's Field. Then we shall see who is stronger!" Big Wolf laughed again. "I will be there, and when I am done with you, you will be in my tummy too!"

Later that night, Buzaak Chinie prepared two big jugs of milk for the blacksmith. She took the milk to the blacksmith and asked him to sharpen her horns for the fight with Big Wolf. The blacksmith sharpened Buzaak Chinie's horns until they were as sharp as knives.

Big Wolf also paid a visit to the blacksmith. "Here is a jug of milk," He said to the blacksmith. "Now, can you sharpen my teeth so they will cut Buzaak Chinie to pieces?" The blacksmith took the jug but something felt wrong. He took the lid off and found that it was a jug filled with dirt. Shaking his head at the Wolf's treachery, the blacksmith pretended to sharpen Big Wolf's teeth. When the blacksmith was done, he told Big Wolf, "You have new teeth. They may feel like cotton, but they are as sharp as knives."

When morning came, Buzaak Chinie and Big Wolf met on Warrior's Field. All about them were strewn the bones of the ancient animal warriors. All the animals of the forest were there as well, looking on from the safety of the forests' edge. Buzaak Chinie called out to Big Wolf, "Are you ready to give me back my kids without a fight?" Big Wolf yelled back, "Not until I sink this set of teeth into some goat meat!" He charged at Buzaak Chinie full speed. Big Wolf leaped on Buzaak Chinie's back and bit her, but as he did, he gasped in horror as his new "teeth" tumbled to the ground. The night before, the blacksmith had pulled out all of Big Wolf's teeth and replaced them with corn seeds!

Before Big Wolf could make another move, Buzaak Chinie, with her razor-sharp horns, cut open his belly with one move of her head. Big Wolf fell upon Warrior's Field as Clumsy, Stubby, and Whiney leaped out into the sunlight, not daring to look back.

Buzaak Chinie gathered up her kids and took them home. She knew they learned a valuable lesson never to open the door for a stranger again. She was so pleased that they were safe, and that night they enjoyed a celebration feast together.

23

About the Author

I was born in Kabul, Afghanistan, on June 10, 1972. As a kid I loved to hear stories told by my great aunt, my mother, and my grandmother, and would retell these tales to my cousins and friends. These were stories without endings. I looked forward to my aunt's visits to hear what happened to the man who walked over seven mountains to face the giant; or the prince who had a mole on his face because of a curse; or the old lady who wanted to get married again at age of ninety.

photo by Haris Rahimi

Of these stories, my favorite was the story of Buzaak Chinie (The Porcelain Goat), Araqchin Tella (The Golden Throw Blanket), Ali Banna Geer (Ali the Complainer), and Seebi Khal Dar (The Apple with Mole).

My father noticed my passion and always brought a new book for me and helped me to read it. My father vanished when I was six years old during the start of the Russian invasion. The government was getting rid of anyone who could stand up for people's rights. My mom felt it was no longer safe for us to be in the country. She tried to find my father for three years, looking into every jail or gulag that prisoners and war victims were kept, but with no luck.

In 1982 we escaped from Afghanistan to Pakistan. It took two years before we could finally come to the United States. I started school as a sixth grader with no knowledge of English. Going through difficulties to earn a living and go to school paid off. I discovered I could draw and I changed my major from Computer Science to Graphic Design / Fine Arts.

I began this project in 1999. I have always admired the illustrations in the stories of the books my father brought for me to read. These were all imported and translated into Dari from other countries for the Afghan children. We did not have any illustrated book to go with the traditional stories that were passed from one generation to the other.

As an Afghan woman, I made a promise to myself that one day I would reveal these wonderful stories and illustrate the cultural beauty of Afghanistan to Americans and to the Afghan children who have been deprived of this beautiful and imaginative part of their culture.

A percentage of the sales of this book will be used to reprint Buzaak Chinie in Dari for children in Afghanistan.

Special thanks to Chris Robyn, Cynthia Baird, Salma Sami, and my Family and Friends.